Feb 18

The Selkie's Mate
Published in Great Britain in 2017
by Graffeg Limited

Written by Nicola Davies
copyright © 2017.
Illustrated by Claire Jenkins
copyright © 2017.
Designed and produced by Graffeg
Limited copyright © 2017

Graffeg Limited, 24 Stradey Park
Business Centre, Mwrwg Road,
Llangennech, Llanelli, Carmarthenshire
SA14 8YP Wales UK
Tel 01554 824000 www.graffeg.com

ISBN 9781910862490

1 2 3 4 5 6 7 8 9

NICOLA DAVIES
THE SELKIE'S MATE

ILLUSTRATION CLAIRE JENKINS

for Emma Corfield

GRAFFEG

THE SELKIE'S MATE

In the far north west are islands where the sea
and land melt into each other in a fretwork of
rocks and water. It's hard to tell salt from fresh,
sand from stone, water from sky. The landscape
shifts from liquid to solid in little more than a
step. The people who live there shift too, from
making a living on land, to the ocean, and back
again. Whether a person is on the sea or the land
depends on the state of the tide, the racing of the
clouds or the weather of their heart. Even the seals
are not always seals, but sometimes selkies, beings
who can slip off their skins, to walk on land in
human form.

In this place lived a young crofter. Like all
crofters, he had a cottage with deep stone walls,
and a thatch of grass, held down with ropes and
pebble-weights, crouched low to resist the winter
gales. He had a garden to grow potatoes, walled
against the wind, a field of flowers for his cow, and

a boat for fishing. Of the three, it was the boat he favoured.

Only the very worst storms kept him ashore. Summer and winter he launched his boat from the crescent of white sand before his croft. He would dance his boat between the rocks and islets, to gaze down into the forest world of weed and fish and cry aloud with joy to dolphins riding the tide race. Seals he loved most of all. He watched their shadows pass beneath his keel and greeted them where they hauled out on rocks and sandbanks to rest at low tide. When they slipped back into the water as the waves rose, he wondered what it would be like to live so easily in two worlds. At night he slept with his window open. Even in his sleep he smiled to hear the sound of the waves and the piping calls of the wading birds coming up the beach with the tide.

The crofter was happy in his life, with the sea in all her moods, from the black breakers of winter with spray-streamed tops, to the silk blue calms of summer. And yet, and yet, something in his heart was yearning, though he could not have said what for. And when the yearning was worst and pulled his heart like a boat dragging its anchor, he would sit on the rocks and sing to the sound of the sea. He sang of the clear green pools, the sunlight shooting through the water and the wide blue promise of the horizon. While the sun left the sky, the stars and moon rose in the velvet night and the waves sighed, he sang on and on. And at last, sometimes close to dawn, he would be comforted, and sleep a little before it was time for the work of the day.

One spring night, when the yearning took him badly, the moon was almost full. It hung yellow as a lamp in the ocean of sky and, as he sang, another voice began to sing with him. Not a human voice, but a seal, hauled out on a sandbank in the middle of the bay. He saw her silver silhouette picked out in moonlight.

Her voice was lovely, so haunting, he felt in it the same unnamed longing that left his own heart awash. He closed his eyes and let his voice wander in harmony with the seal's.

The crofter was entirely lost in the kinship of their singing and only knew that hours had passed when the tide came up and washed both himself and the seal from their dry places.

Every night as the moon blossomed to fullness,

like a flower in the velvet sky, the crofter sang
and the seal came and sang with him. All day, out
in his boat he thought of how it felt when their
voices melted together. All day, he waited for the
moonlight and the singing to begin again.

But on the seventh night, as the moon began
to wane and wither, the seal did not come.
The crofter sat on the rocks singing, until his
throat was empty and the tide came up. The dark
faded into a kind of pale oblivion as the sky grew
light in the dawn. And still she never came.

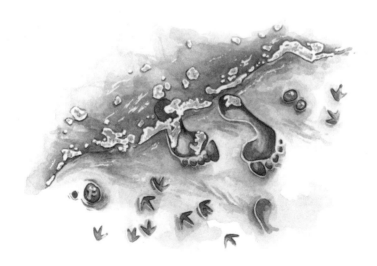

Stiff and hoarse and sore he rose from his place. He walked along the shore and knew at last the name of the longing he'd sung; it was loneliness, and it lay in his heart like a cold, cold stone. For the first time in his life the crofter felt that his solitariness was a burden to him.

At that moment, the sun rose over the hill and as its first rays fell on the roof of his bothy, a silver voice, a human voice, rang out from his very own doorway! There, standing on the threshold of his home, was the loveliest woman he'd ever seen, her skin and hair shining in the sun like the silvery sea. She smiled him such a welcome, something that he'd never had in all his life before.

In her arms she held a folded sealskin, as soft and silvered as she was herself.

"Here is my selkie skin," she said, giving it to him, "you must keep it safe from all harm, and whenever I ask for it, you must give it me back, so I may be free to return from where I came, if I choose."

He nodded his agreement to their bargain and she took his hand in hers and led him inside.

꩜

Such a plain thing to say that they were happy, but that is what they were. Their voices and their lives in harmony. Happy on the sea out in the bay, catching fish and pulling crabs from pots. Happy too on the land. The Selkie's delight in the novelty of earth and air gave the crofter a new love of his garden and his field. Planting potatoes together in their little field became a wonder to him. He laughed to see her run the sandy soil through her fingers like so much gold dust. When she rested her silver head against his cow's side at milking time, he couldn't take his gaze away. Bringing in the sweet hay to the barn with her was like a sacrament.

By the fire when the cold came, or even holding down the thatch in a ripping gale, they smiled together. Seasons passed, each glowing like a yellow moon, and in time they rocked their twin babies in the cradles that the crofter carved from driftwood.

For seven years they were happy and then, one spring day, the Selkie turned to her crofter and said,

"Will you give me my skin?"

The crofter's heart stood still in his chest. In his mind he searched the days and weeks to find a reason, some hurt he'd done her, but could find none. His voice died in his throat. Somehow he managed a smile and an answer.

"Tomorrow."

All that night, while his Selkie slept, he searched under the starlight for the loveliest shells. And when that tomorrow came, instead of the sealskin, he gave her a necklace made of the pink cowries and sunset tellin shells that he'd gathered on the shore.

She took the necklace and laid it on the table without a word, and went to tend their children.

Weeks passed. The corncrake grated his song from the corner of the hayfield and the redshank piped from the gatepost of the garden. Flowers bloomed. Gannets flung themselves like rash arrows into the bay. The air was full of cries, oystercatchers and curlews, plovers and larks. But in the space between the crofter and his Selkie, silence fell.

The crofter tried to forget the Selkie's request, but always, it lay between them. And then, one morning as they hauled their nets out in the bay, she asked a second time.

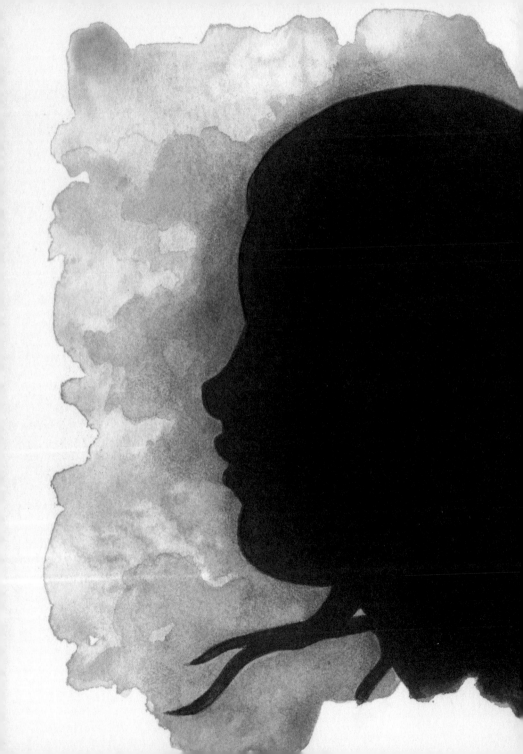

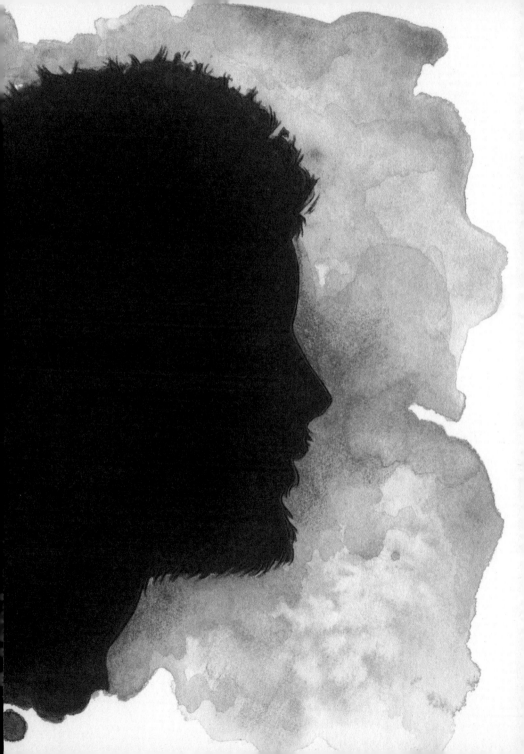

"Will you give me my skin?"

And again he searched his mind for some mistake he'd made. Finding nothing, he smiled an empty smile and answered her,

'Tomorrow."

He scoured the beach for driftwood. All night he worked, carving shapes into the silver grain. And when that tomorrow came, instead of the sealskin, he gave her a rocking chair carved with fish and flowers, birds and dolphins, creatures of both worlds. She hardly looked at it and turned

from him to go out and milk the cow.

The summer swelled with sun and sweetness. The sea was calm and kind, the children laughed and made seashell patterns on the sand. Inside his heart, the crofter held his breath and hoped. But then one evening, when the sun sank in a purple haze over the sea, his Selkie asked a third time,

"Will you give me my skin?"

He took a beat to find his voice but smiled again his false smile. But this time when he answered her 'tomorrow', she told him that she wanted no more gifts, and turned away.

His Selkie didn't ask again. The shine of her grew dull, like a fish out of water. She watched her crofter now, from a distance, so she might find where he had hidden her skin. The crofter grew careful, wily, hiding the skin in a different place each night. He looked at his Selkie and saw now all her otherness. He began to shun his own son and daughter so they would have nothing to tell their mother about her skin.

The strain of it, the watching and the hiding, wore their happiness to nothing. It wore away their singing and their harmony.

So it went on. The fish caught. The garden planted. The cow milked. The hay brought in. And all of it without joy, or love, or singing. Only the two children thrived and grew and blossomed, and sometimes made their mother smile, so she would show a flash of silver for a moment, like a herring in a net. Seeing that, the crofter's heart wrenched with longing and he'd turn his face away, back to his nets, or his digging.

As the children grew tall and strong they helped their mother and their father. They filled the silence that lay between their parents, so that sometimes the little white cottage on the shore rang with song, and was almost happy. But still their mother's silver flashed only ever for a moment, and then their father's face would always turn away. Sometimes the children, too, were full with a longing that they could not name.

Then one year, at haymaking, the children saw the crofter put something into the heart of the first stook. It was folded, sleek and shining, like smoothed hair. They looked at each other, mystified and yet somehow delighted. What was that beautiful thing that reminded them of their mother's happiest smile? But their father's furtive looks told them it was not for them to find. They looked at each other and did not speak, all at once a little afraid.

That night their mother came to them in their bedroom among the eaves, as she hadn't done since they were very small. She sat with them, talking, listening, humming. Both children felt that they had, for a moment, returned to that sweet, lost time, when their mother shone like the sea. As they floated between the worlds of dream and waking, they thought they heard her ask a question,

"Have you seen my skin? My silvery skin?" Both knew at once that they had the answer. Half sleeping the girl breathed,

"In the stook."

Almost dreaming the boy whispered,

"Yes, the first stook of summer!"

Then they turned their heads to the pillow and closed their eyes.

For a long, long time their mother stroked their hair and let her silver tears fall on their lips, salt as the ocean. She kissed them for the last time, and went out into the glowing dusk amongst the stooks of hay.

All night the children dreamed of seaweed forests, sparkling shoals of sprats, and shooting lines of sunlight. They dreamed selkie dreams and in them swam immersed in their mother's silvery happiness.

At daybreak the crofter woke from a dream of singing. He kept his eyes closed to hold onto the joy of it. For the first time in many years his head was clear and light, full of the jewel blue of sea and sky. Through the open window came the sea sounds, comforting him as they had used to do long ago. The crofter sighed and reached out to find his Selkie's hand.

The bed beside him was empty and quite cold.
Lying on the driftwood rocking chair on which
no one had ever sat, was the string of cowries and
sunset shells. From the barn, the cow lowed un-
milked.

He ran out and up into the hayfield, where
the corncrake still grated his cry in the uncut
edges. There, at the top of the field, where the
bay showed blue over the low stone wall, the first
stook was torn to pieces. He searched through the
scattered grasses, dotted with the withered seed
heads of spring's flowers, but he knew he would
find nothing.

He ran to the shore where he and his Selkie had
so often launched their little boat. It was glassy
calm. Small wavelets whispered onto the sand.
The sea was like his Selkie, sleeping, sighing,
shining, silver at his side and the crofters heart
turned like the tide within him. He understood,
too late, that she had trusted him with her

freedom, and he had failed her. He stood in the morning sun and sang and sang and sang, until he was empty of all his tears.

Every day of her life the Selkie left fish of all kinds and colours on the shore for her children. And when the full moon shone on the bay she'd lie on the sandbank at low tide, and blend her voice in sweetness and in longing, with her crofter, her lost love.

Nicola Davies

Nicola is an award-winning author, whose many books for children include *The Promise* (Green Earth Book Award 2015, CILIP Kate Greenaway Medal Shortlist 2015), *Tiny* (AAAS/Subaru SB&F Prize 2015), *A First Book of Nature*, *Whale Boy* (Blue Peter Book Awards Shortlist 2014), and the Heroes of the Wild series (Portsmouth Book Award 2014).

She graduated in Zoology, studied whales and bats and then worked for the BBC Natural History Unit. Underlying all Nicola's writing is the belief that a relationship with nature is essential to every human being, and that now, more than ever, we need to renew that relationship.

Nicola's children's books from Graffeg include *Perfect*, the Shadows and Light series, *The Word Bird*, *Animal Surprises* and *Into the Blue*.

Claire Jenkins

Claire Jenkins is an illustration graduate from Swansea, South Wales.

Working in pencil, markers or watercolour, she is inspired by her surroundings, producing artwork that includes portraiture as well as the natural world.

The Selkie's Mate is the first book she has illustrated.

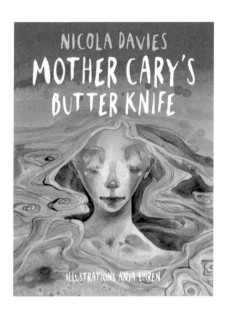

" Out of the low slung car a tall, ancient man unfurled himself. His eyes were blue-green, like a backlit wave, his face as craggy as the coast, and topped with a tower of foam-white hair. When the man spoke, his voice was as commanding as storm waves breaking in a cave.

"The sea looks fair tonight, does it not?" he said. Keenan opened his mouth to reply but found his own voice entirely missing. The strange man growled on, and raised a warning finger before the boy's wide eyes. "

The smallest of three brothers, Keenan Mowat had a priceless talent: he loved the sea and the sea loved him right back...

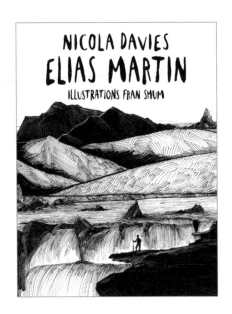

NICOLA DAVIES
ELIAS MARTIN
ILLUSTRATIONS FRAN SHUM

By the time he washed up to the door of a one-roomed log cabin, in the remote backwoods of a northern province, he knew this was his last chance in life. He carried a fur trapper's licence, a bag of steel traps, a rifle and the conviction that all of nature was his personal enemy. He was seventeen years old.

Trawling the north, looking for his last chance of survival, Elias Martin lives a scowling, solitary life for a decade until a small, lost child wanders into his path.

In the days before computers, before cars, before electricity in wires or water in taps, or food in supermarkets, before even roads and writing, people lived by what they could get from the land. Humans were closer to nature, at the mercy of the cold and wind, floods and drought, as other animals were. Back then, humans and animals were fellow beings under the sky. Perhaps that's why it seemed possible, back then, for humans to change into animals, and animals into humans.

Back then, humans and animals were fellow beings under the sky. Perhaps that's why it seemed possible for humans to change into animals.

Graffeg Children's Books

The White Hare
Nicola Davies
Illustrated by Anastasia Izlesou

Mother Cary's Butter Knife
Nicola Davies
Illustrations by Anja Uhren

Elias Martin
Nicola Davies
Illustrations by Fran Shum

The Selkie's Mate
Nicola Davies
Illustrations by Claire Jenkins

Bee Boy and the Moonflowers
Nicola Davies

The Eel Question
Nicola Davies

The Word Bird
Nicola Davies
Illustrations by Abbie Cameron

Animal Surprises
Nicola Davies
Illustrations by Abbie Cameron

Into the Blue
Nicola Davies
Illustrations by Abbie Cameron

Perfect
Nicola Davies
Illustrations by Cathy Fisher
"Written with gentle sensitivity and
stunningly illustrated" *Daily Mail*

Cooks & Kids 3
Edited by Gregg Wallace

Small Finds a Home

Celestine and the Hare

Paper Boat for Panda

Celestine and the Hare

Honey for Tea

Celestine and the Hare

Catching Dreams

Celestine and the Hare

A Small Song

Celestine and the Hare

Finding Your Place

Celestine and the Hare

"Life-affirming books that encourage us all
to nurture the playfulness of childhood"
Playing by the Book